Molly

Chapter 1 ❋
The Warm-Up

What a lovely morning. The sun was shining. The birds were singing. And my pony, Norton, was waiting for me.

I knew Norton just couldn't wait to be saddled up for a ride. I love Norton, and Norton loves me. He is the best pony in the world, and he has the best rider – me!

Sometimes other people don't see how
wonderful Norton is. That judge at the
last show wasn't very good. It wasn't
Norton's fault that she stood in his way
and he knocked her over.

Then the judge made a huge mistake. She gave the blue ribbon to Jillian Jones, the rider with the skinny pony. She should have given it to me and Norton.

What a disaster!

"Come here, Norty," I shouted. "Time to practise for the next show. We're definitely going to win this time."

Sometimes when Norton is eating he doesn't hear me. He must be a very loud muncher.

Norton loves to be with me. He is only really happy when he is carrying me on his back.

We have wonderful adventures, Norton and I.

"Come here, buddy. I bet you can't
wait to have this halter on you. Come
here, champ. Hey, Norton, you're going
the wrong way," I cried.

Norton likes to warm up before we go for a ride. He is so clever. Sometimes I forget about the warm-up.

"Great warm-up, Norton. Now come and get your halter on," I said.

But Norton must have been eating again because he didn't hear me.

It took me forever to get Norton's attention. I finally crept up beside him and rubbed his ears. Then I tried to slip the halter over his nose.

"Ouch!" I yelled.

Norton stepped on my foot. I know it was an accident, because only a naughty pony would do that on purpose. And my Norton was not naughty!

In fact, Norton felt so bad about the accident that he ran away.

"Wait, Norton, wait!" I called out. But Norton was so embarrassed he just couldn't face me.

Chapter 2

Think Like a Horse

I know a lot about horses. I've got
plenty of horse books at home. Horses are
flight animals. That means that when
they roamed the plains in the wild, they
would run at just a hint of danger.

It is my job as Norton's trainer to let him know there is nothing to fear. I have to be calm and patient at all times.

Then I lost sight of Norton.

"Norton, where are you?" I called out.

Sometimes Norton likes to play
hide-and-seek.

"Okay, you win, Norton,"
I said. "You can come out now."

Sometimes a horse will test its trainer's patience. That's when I remind myself that Norton is just an animal, and I am in charge.

Norton cannot outsmart me.

I tried to think like a horse. I tried to think like Norton. Where would I go if I were hiding from my wonderful, caring owner?

I was still thinking when I heard a twig snap. I have incredibly good hearing. Norton was nearby.

"I'm counting, Norton. Eight, nine, ten. Here I come, ready or not!" I yelled.

Norton was scared. He must have thought I was some kind of horse-eating monster.

"No, Norton, wait!" I cried out.

But it was too late. Norton ran away with the speed of a racehorse.

As I watched Norton, I saw that he was heading for the fence.

"Stop, Norton, no!" I cried out.

Not only was Norton a powerful racing machine, he was thinking of becoming a jumping machine as well.

"No!" I commanded.

Sometimes I have to be really strict
with Norton. When I put on my special
in-charge voice, Norton does what I say.
So when I said "no," Norton stopped
running.

Of course, it helped that I had my emergency sugar cube. Norton can never refuse a treat.

"Come here, Norton. Look what I have for you. That's a good pony. Come to Molly for a big surprise," I said calmly.

Norton took a step closer. Then
another. If I got his halter on now, there
would still be time for a quick trot . . .
OUCH!

"Norton, it's rude to snatch," I scolded. "Where are you going?"

Norton had taken my only sugar cube. It wasn't his fault I didn't have another one. As a trainer, you must always be alert. I have to keep reminding myself of this.

❋ Chapter 3 ❋
Apple Season

When things don't go as planned, a good trainer will always have a back-up plan. It was time to show Norton exactly who was in charge.

Lucky for me, it was apple season.
Norton loved apples. I picked the two
best apples on a nearby apple tree.
One to set the trap, and the other as
a backup.

I showed Norton the apple, and he came quietly without a fight.

"Good boy," I said, giving him a pat.

Apple juice dribbled off Norton's chin as I slipped the halter over his head. He nudged my pocket. Norton's clever nose had found my backup apple.

I was finally going to get my ride.

"Norton, what you need is some quality training," I told him.

But when I grabbed the rope, it was
all slippery with apple juice and pony
slobber. Norton pulled away, and the
rope slipped right through my fingers.

Chapter 4

Today's Lesson

"Please come back, Norton. You'll get tangled up in the rope and fall," I yelled.

But Norton was gone again.

A good horse trainer will never cry. Never ever. The most important thing is not to leave before your pony has learned the day's lesson. Today's lesson was that I was in charge.

I had another trick I could use. And this time, I wouldn't let go of the rope when Norton got close to me. I would catch that pony if it took me a whole week.

"That's right, Norton," I said. "Look what I have for you. Better than sugar. Better than apples."

Norton's ears pricked with excitement when I shook the bucket. He could hear those plump, sweet, delicious oats rattling inside his food bucket.

"Norton, if you want the oats, you must promise to be a good pony. No more running away," I said.

Norton walked over to me and nudged my arm.

I tied Norton up very tightly so he
could not escape again. I watched him as
he stuffed his nose deep into the bucket
of oats.

I couldn't be angry with Norton. He
just loves to fool around. That's what
makes him so loveable.

By the time Norton finished his oats,
it was too late to ride. The moon cast
big shadows on the ground. I wondered
what it would be like to be Molly the
Moonlight Rider.

"Molly! Dinner!" Mum yelled from the house.

Slowly, I unbuckled Norton's halter.

A good trainer knows when to give up and call it a day.

"Tomorrow, Norton," I told my pony. "Tomorrow we will practise for the show."

I knew Norton was excited to get saddled up for a ride. Norton loves me, and I love Norton. He is the best pony in the world.

And he has the best trainer and rider in the world – me!

The End

GETTING TO KNOW YOUR PONY

To safely ride or even approach a pony, make sure it is comfortable around you. Remember these tips while making friends with a pony.

1 **NEVER APPROACH FROM BEHIND.** You could get kicked! Don't approach head-on either. A pony cannot see directly in front of it. Try approaching from an angle.

2 **BE FRIENDLY TO BUILD TRUST.** As you walk towards the pony, hold out your hand. Use a soft voice to talk to the pony.

3 **TREAT YOUR PONY TO SOMETHING SPECIAL.** A pony will usually come to you if you have food. Ponies especially like carrots and apples. If you hold your palm out flat when offering a treat, the pony's teeth cannot grab your skin.

4 **STAY CALM AND PATIENT.** Never chase a pony or give it a reason to be afraid of you. Quick movements or yelling will only frighten it.

5 **FIGURE OUT HOW THE PONY IS FEELING.** Look at its ears and face. If it is angry, it will point its ears back and flare its nostrils. If it is scared, it will also roll its eyes until the white parts show. That is a good sign to stay away!

ABOUT THE AUTHOR

While growing up, Bernadette Kelly desperately wanted her own horse. Although she rode other people's horses, she didn't get one of her own until she was a grown-up. Many years later, she is still obsessed with horses. Luckily, she lives in the country where there is plenty of room for her four-legged friends. When she's not writing or working with her horses, Bernadette takes her two children to pony club competitions.

ABOUT THE ILLUSTRATOR

Liz Alger loves horses so much that she left suburbia to live in the rambling outskirts of Melbourne, Australia. Her new home provided plenty of room to indulge in her passion. Her love of animals, horses in particular, shines through in the delightful and humorous illustrations of Norton, the naughty pony in the *Pony Tales* series.

GLOSSARY

halter a set of straps enclosing an animal's head. A rope or strap for leading may be attached to the halter.

horse show a place where people show their horses to judges. Horses are judged on looks, obedience, and ability.

oats a type of grain that is fed to horses

racehorse a type of horse that is trained specifically for racing

trainer a person who teaches horses to listen to commands

trot when a horse goes faster than walking but is not quite running

DISCUSSION QUESTIONS

1. Do you think Norton is naughty or clever? Explain your answer.

2. What could Molly do differently so Norton would listen to her?

3. If you had a horse, what would you name it? Why?

WRITING PROMPTS

1. Molly and Norton like to go on adventures. If you had a horse, what kind of adventures would you go on? Write a paragraph describing your adventures.

2. How would you get Norton to listen? Write down at least five rules you would have Norton follow.

3. Even when Norton doesn't listen, Molly loves him. He is her best friend. Write a paragraph about your best friend.

Take Another Ride with Norton

Norton is a naughty pony. Everyone thinks so.
Well, everyone except his owner, Molly. She thinks
Norton is the most perfect pony in the whole
world, no matter what kind of trouble he causes!

Pony Tales

978 1 4062 6635 1

978 1 4062 6633 7

978 1 4062 6634 4